THIS BOOK
BELONGS TO

. . . .

Illustrations by Priscilla Lamont

Every effort has been made to trace the ownership of all material. In the event of any question arising as to the use of the material, the publisher will be happy to make the necessary correction for use in future printings.

This edition published by Parragon in 2013
Parragon
Chartist House
15–17 Trim Street
Bath BA1 1HA, UK
www.parragon.com

ISBN 978-1-4723-2276-0

Printed in China

NurSery RhYme TreAsury

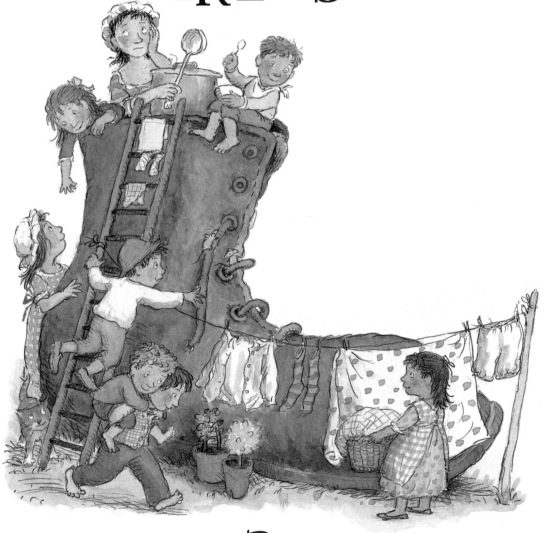

PaRragon

Bath · New York · Singapore · Hong Kong · Cologne · Delhi
Melbourne · Amsterdam · Johannesburg · Shenzhen

Contents

Counting Rhymes

Action Rhymes

Food Rhymes

Animal Rhymes

Nonsense Rhymes

Playground Rhymes

Bedtime Rhymes

Classic Rhymes

Humpty Dumpty

Humpty Dumpty sat on a wall,
Humpty Dumpty had a great fall;
All the king's horses, and all the king's men
Couldn't put Humpty together again!

Jack and Jill

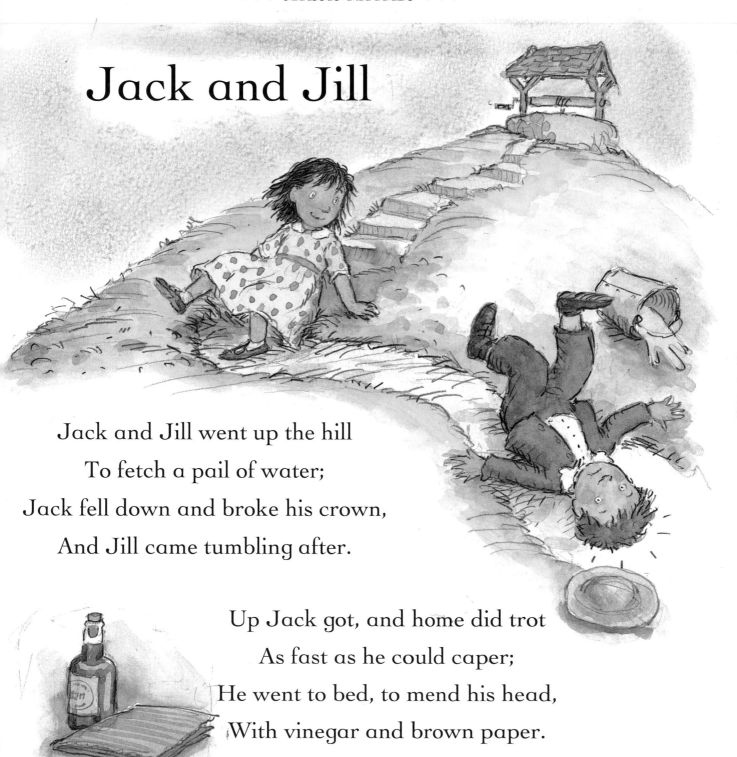

Jack and Jill went up the hill
To fetch a pail of water;
Jack fell down and broke his crown,
And Jill came tumbling after.

Up Jack got, and home did trot
As fast as he could caper;
He went to bed, to mend his head,
With vinegar and brown paper.

The Grand Old Duke of York

The grand old Duke of York,
He had ten thousand men,
He marched them up to the top of the hill,
And he marched them down again.

When they were up, they were up,

And when they were down, they were down,

And when they were only half way up,

They were neither up nor down.

Mary, Mary, Quite Contrary

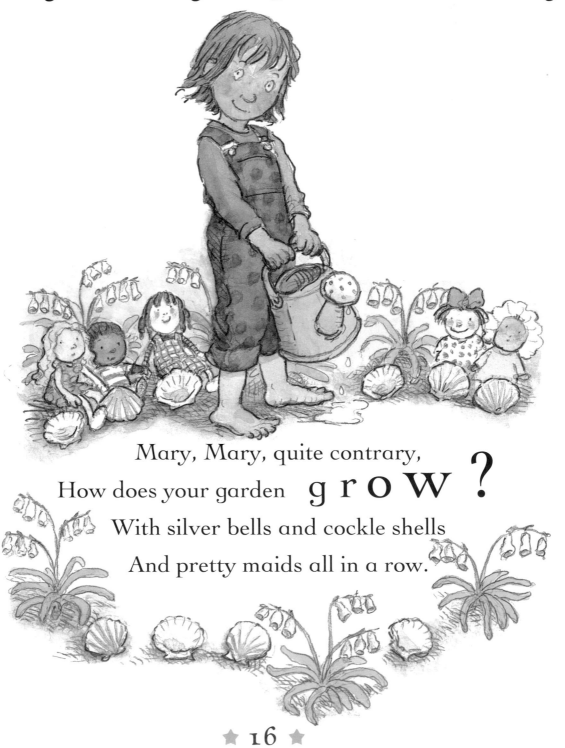

Mary, Mary, quite contrary,

How does your garden g r o w ?

With silver bells and cockle shells

And pretty maids all in a row.

There Was a Little Girl

There was a little girl,
And she had a little curl,
Right in the middle
Of her forehead.

When she was good,
She was very, very good,
But when she was bad,
She was HORRID.

Doctor Foster

Doctor Foster

Went to Gloucester

In a shower of rain;

He stepped in a puddle,

Right up to his middle,

And never went there again!

Rain, Rain, Go Away

Rain, rain, go away,

Come again another day.

Little Johnny wants to play.

One Misty, Moisty Morning

One misty, moisty morning,
When cloudy was the weather,
There I met an old man
All clothed in leather.
He began to compliment
And I began to grin;
How do you do?
And how do you do?
And how do you do
AGAIN?

Little Miss Muffet

Little Miss Muffet
Sat on a tuffet,
Eating her curds and whey;

Along came a spider,

Who sat down beside her

And frightened Miss Muffet away.

Rub a Dub Dub

Rub a dub dub,

Three men in a tub,

And how do you think they got there?

The butcher, the baker,

The candlestick maker,

They all jumped out

    of a rotten potato,

It was enough to make

    a man stare.

Cobbler, Cobbler, Mend My Shoe

Cobbler, cobbler, mend my shoe.

Get it done by half past two.

Half past two is much too late!

Get it done by half past eight.

See-Saw, Margery Daw

See-saw, Margery Daw,

Johnny shall have a new master;

He shall have but a penny a day,

Because he can't work any faster.

There Was an Old Woman Who Lived in a Shoe

There was an old woman
who lived in a shoe.
She had so many children
she didn't know what to do!
So she gave them some broth
without any bread;
And she whipped them all soundly
and sent them to bed.

Tom, Tom, the Piper's Son

Tom, Tom, the piper's son,

Stole a pig and away he ran.

The pig was eat, and Tom was beat,

And Tom went roaring down the street.

Old King Cole

Old King Cole was a merry old soul,
and a merry old soul was he;
He called for his pipe in the middle of the night,
And he called for his fiddlers three.

Every fiddler had a very fine fiddle,
and a very fine fiddle had he;
Oh there's none so rare as can compare,
With King Cole and his fiddlers three.

Hector Protector

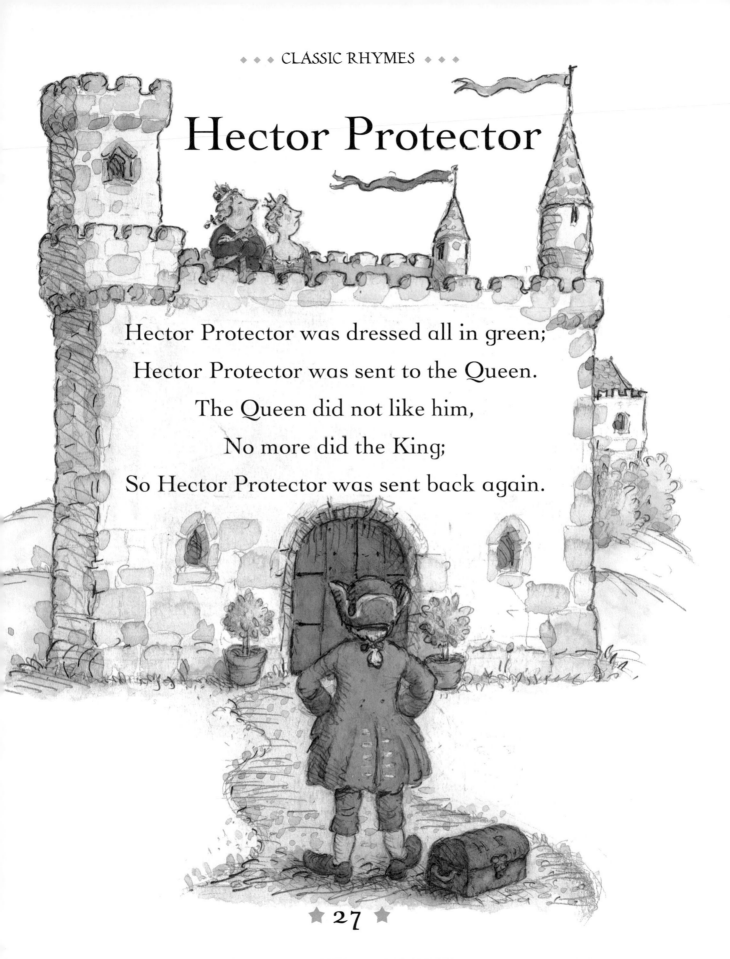

Hector Protector was dressed all in green;

Hector Protector was sent to the Queen.

The Queen did not like him,

No more did the King;

So Hector Protector was sent back again.

Monday's Child

Monday's child is fair of face,

Tuesday's child is full of grace,

Wednesday's child is full of woe,

Thursday's child has far to go,

Friday's child is loving and giving,

Saturday's child works hard for his living,

And the child that is born on the Sabbath day

Is bonny and blithe and good and gay.

Solomon Grundy

Solomon Grundy,
Born on a Monday,
Christened on Tuesday,

Married on Wednesday,
Took ill on Thursday,
Grew worse on Friday,

Died on Saturday,
Buried on Sunday.
That was the end of
Solomon Grundy.

Polly, Put the Kettle On

Polly, put the kettle on,
Polly, put the kettle on,
Polly, put the kettle on,
We'll all have tea.

Sukey, take it off again,
Sukey, take it off again,
Sukey, take it off again,
They've all gone away.

Coffee and Tea

Molly, my sister, and I fell out,

And what do you think it was all about?

She loved coffee and I loved tea,

And that was the reason we couldn't agree.

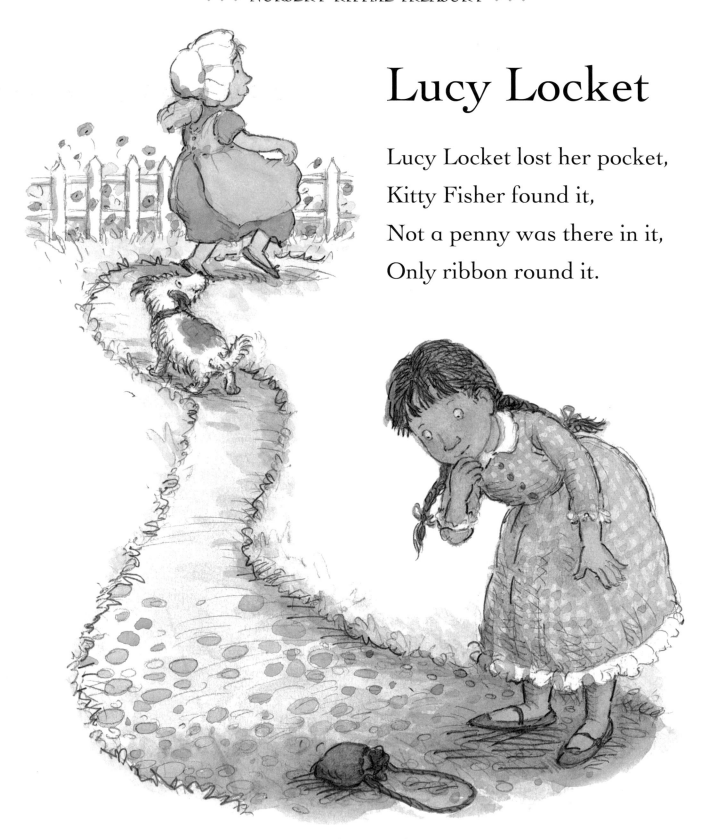

Lucy Locket

Lucy Locket lost her pocket,
Kitty Fisher found it,
Not a penny was there in it,
Only ribbon round it.

A-Tisket A-Tasket

A-tisket a-tasket,

A green and yellow basket.

I wrote a letter to my love,

And on the way I dropped it.

I dropped it, I dropped it,

And on the way I dropped it.

A little boy picked it up,

And put it in his pocket.

Lavender's Blue

Lavender's blue, dilly, dilly,
Lavender's green;
When I am king, dilly, dilly,
You shall be queen.

Counting

Rhymes

A was an Apple Pie

A was an apple pie,
B bit it,
C cut it,
D dealt it,
E eat it,

F fought for it,
G got it,
H had it,
I inspected it,

J jumped for it,
K kept it,
L longed for it,
M mourned for it,

N nodded at it,
O opened it,
P peeped in it,
Q quartered it,

R ran for it,
S stole it,
T took it,
U upset it,

V viewed it,
W wanted it,
X, Y, Z,
All wished for
a piece in hand.

Each Peach, Pear, Plum

Each peach, pear, plum,

Out goes Tom Thumb;

Tom Thumb won't do,

Out goes Betty Blue;

Betty Blue won't go,

So out goes you.

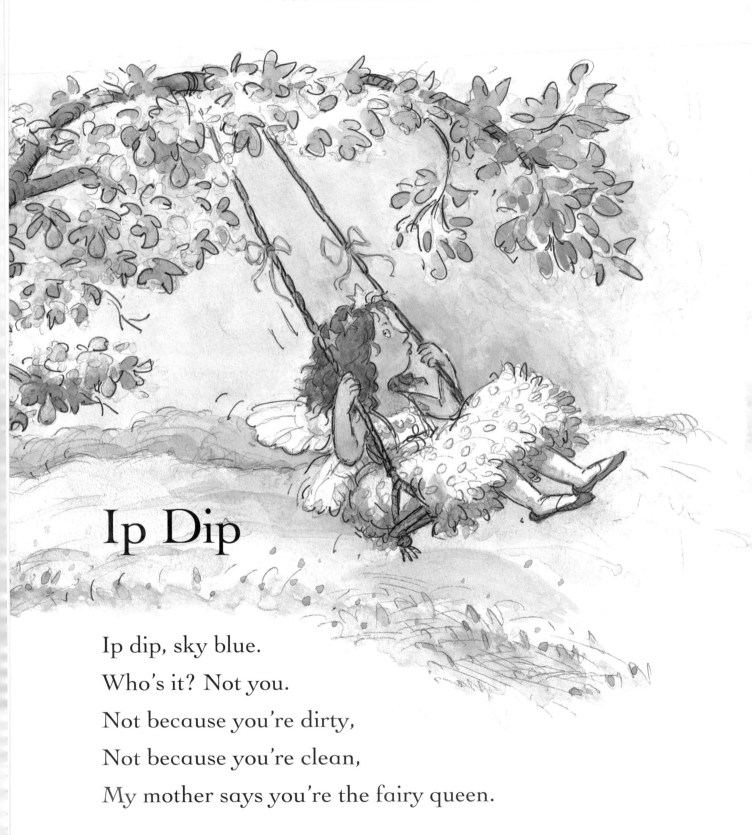

Ip Dip

Ip dip, sky blue.

Who's it? Not you.

Not because you're dirty,

Not because you're clean,

My mother says you're the fairy queen.

One Man Went to Mow

One man went to mow,

Went to mow a meadow,

One man, and his dog,

Went to mow a meadow.

Two men went to mow,

Went to mow a meadow,

Two men, one man, and his dog,

Went to mow a meadow.

Three men went to mow,
Went to mow a meadow,
Three men, two men,
one man, and his dog,
Went to mow a meadow.

Four men went to mow,
Went to mow a meadow,
Four men, three men, two men,
one man, and his dog,
Went to mow a meadow.

You can keep adding verses as far as you can count.

One, Two, Buckle My Shoe

One, two, buckle my shoe;

Three, four, knock at the door;

Five, six, pick up sticks;

Seven, eight, lay them straight;

Nine, ten, a big fat hen;

Eleven, twelve, dig and delve;

Thirteen, fourteen, maids a-courting;

Fifteen, sixteen, maids in the kitchen;

Seventeen, eighteen, maids in waiting;

Nineteen, twenty, my plate's empty!

Five Little Ducks

Five little ducks went swimming one day,
Over the hills and far away.
Mother duck said, "Quack, quack, quack, quack,"
But only four little ducks came back.

Four little ducks went swimming one day
Over the hills and far away.
Mother duck said, "Quack, quack, quack, quack,"
But only three little ducks came back.

Three little ducks went swimming one day
Over the hills and far away.
Mother duck said, "Quack, quack, quack, quack,"
But only two little ducks came back.

Two little ducks went swimming one day
Over the hills and far away.
Mother duck said, "Quack, quack, quack, quack,"
But only one little duck came back.

One little duck went swimming one day
Over the hills and far away.
Mother duck said, "Quack, quack, quack, quack,"
But none of the five little ducks came back.

Mother duck went swimming one day
Over the hills and far away.
Mother duck said, "Quack, quack, quack, quack,"
And five little ducks came swimming back.

One, Two, Three, Four, Five

One, two, three, four, five,
Once I caught a fish alive.
Six, seven, eight, nine, ten,
Then I let it go again.

Why did you let it go?
Because it bit my finger so.
Which finger did it bite?
This little finger on the right.

Five Fat Sausages

Five fat sausages sizzling in the pan,
All of a sudden one went BANG!

Four fat sausages sizzling in the pan,
All of a sudden one went BANG!

Three fat sausages sizzling in the pan,
All of a sudden one went BANG!

Two fat sausages sizzling in the pan,
All of a sudden one went BANG!

One fat sausage sizzling in the pan,
All of a sudden it went BANG!

And there were no sausages left!

Five Little Monkeys

Five little monkeys jumping on the bed,

One fell off and bumped his head.

Mama called the Doctor and the Doctor said,

"No more monkeys jumping on the bed!"

Four little monkeys jumping on the bed,

One fell off and bumped her head.

Papa called the Doctor and the Doctor said,

"No more monkeys jumping on the bed!"

Three little monkeys jumping on the bed,

One fell off and bumped his head.

Mama called the Doctor and the Doctor said,

"No more monkeys jumping on the bed!"

Two little monkeys jumping on the bed,

One fell off and bumped her head.

Papa called the Doctor and the Doctor said,

"No more monkeys jumping on the bed!"

One little monkey jumping on the bed,

He fell off and bumped his head.

Mama called the Doctor and the Doctor said,

"Put those monkeys straight to bed!"

One for Sorrow

One for sorrow,
Two for joy,
Three for a girl,
Four for a boy,
Five for silver,
Six for gold,
Seven for a secret
Never to be told.

Tinker, Tailor, Soldier, Sailor

Tinker,

Tailor,

Soldier,

Sailor,

Rich man,

Poor man,

Beggarman,

Thief!

This Old Man

This old man, he played one;

He played knick-knack on a drum.

    Chorus: With a knick-knack, paddy whack,

                Give a dog a bone;

                This old man came rolling home.

This old man, he played two;

He played knick-knack on my shoe.

    Chorus: With a knick-knack, paddy whack,

                Give a dog a bone;

                This old man came rolling home.

This old man, he played three;
He played knick-knack on my knee.
    Chorus: With a knick-knack, paddy whack,
                  Give a dog a bone;
                  This old man came rolling home.

This old man, he played four;
He played knick-knack on my door.
    Chorus: With a knick-knack, paddy whack,
                  Give a dog a bone;
                  This old man came rolling home.

This old man, he played five;
He played knick-knack on my hive.
    Chorus: With a knick-knack, paddy whack,
                  Give a dog a bone;
                  This old man came rolling home.

This old man, he played six;

He played knick-knack on my sticks.

    Chorus: With a knick-knack, paddy whack,

                 Give a dog a bone;

                 This old man came rolling home.

This old man, he played seven;

He played knick-knack up to heaven.

    Chorus

This old man, he played eight;

He played knick-knack on my gate.

    Chorus

This old man, he played nine;

He played knick-knack on my spine.

    Chorus

This old man, he played ten;

He played knick-knack once again.

    Chorus

Action Rhymes

Pat-a-Cake, Pat-a-Cake

Pat-a-cake, pat-a-cake, baker's man,

(Clap in rhythm)

Bake me a cake as fast as you can.

(Clap in rhythm)

Pat it and prick it and mark it with B,

(Pat and 'prick' palm and trace letter B)

And put it in the oven for Baby and me!

(Action of putting cake in oven)

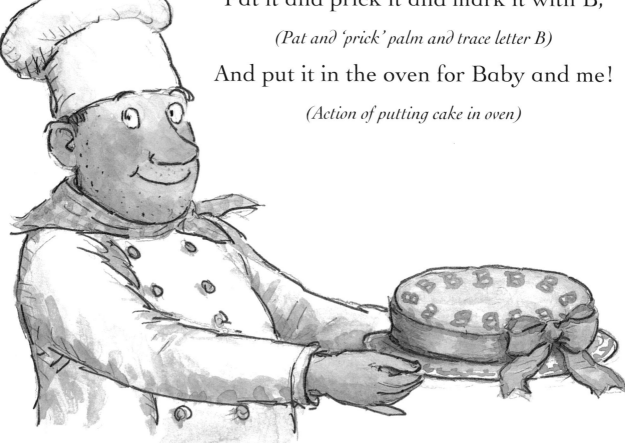

I'm a Little Teapot

I'm a little teapot, short and stout,

Here's my handle, here's my spout.

When I get my steam up hear me shout,

Tip me up and pour me out.

Row, Row, Row Your Boat

(Mime a rowing action throughout as the rhyme suggests)

Row, row, row your boat

Gently down the stream.

Merrily, merrily, merrily, merrily,

Life is but a dream.

Round and Round the Garden

Round and round the garden

Like a teddy bear;

(Draw a circle on the palm of your baby's hand

with your finger)

One step, two steps,

(Walk your fingers up your baby's arm)

Tickle you under there!

(Tickle baby under the arm)

The Wheels on the Bus

The wheels on the bus go
    round and round,
Round and round,
    round and round.
The wheels on the bus go
    round and round,
All day long.

(Move hands in a circular motion)

The wipers on the bus go
    swish, swish, swish!
Swish, swish, swish!
    swish, swish, swish!
The wipers on the bus go
    swish, swish, swish!
All day long.

(Wiggle both index fingers)

The horn on the bus goes

beep, beep, beep!

Beep, beep, beep!

beep, beep, beep!

The horn on the bus goes

beep, beep, beep!

All day long.

(Pretend to press a horn)

The people on the bus go

chat, chat, chat,

Chat, chat, chat,

chat, chat, chat.

The people on the bus go

chat, chat, chat,

All day long.

(Hold your thumb and fingers out straight to make a beak shape and open and close it)

Here is the Church

Here is the church,

(Interlace fingers)

Here is the steeple,

(Put up both pointing fingers to make a steeple)

Look inside…

(Turn both hands over)

And see all the people!

(Wiggle your fingers)

This is the Way

This is the way we wash our hands,
Wash our hands, wash our hands.
This is the way we wash our hands
So early in the morning.

This is the way we wash our face,
Wash our face, wash our face.
This is the way we wash our face
So early in the morning.

This is the way we brush our teeth,
Brush our teeth, brush our teeth.
This is the way we brush our teeth
So early in the morning.

This is the way we comb our hair,
Comb our hair, comb our hair.
This is the way we comb our hair
So early in the morning.

This is the way we wave goodbye,
Wave goodbye, wave goodbye.
This is the way we wave goodbye
So early in the morning.

Ten in the Bed

There were ten in the bed and the little one said,
"Roll over, roll over."

So they all rolled over and one fell out.
There were nine in the bed and the little one said,
"Roll over, roll over."

So they all rolled over and one fell out.
There were eight in the bed and the little one said,
"Roll over, roll over."

So they all rolled over and one fell out.
There were seven in the bed and the little one said,
"Roll over, roll over."

So they all rolled over and one fell out.

There were six in the bed and the little one said,

"Roll over, roll over."

So they all rolled over and one fell out.

There were five in the bed and the little one said,

"Roll over, roll over."

So they all rolled over and one fell out.

There were four in the bed and the little one said,

"Roll over, roll over."

So they all rolled over and one fell out.

There were three in the bed and the little one said,

"Roll over, roll over."

So they all rolled over and one fell out.

There were two in the bed and the little one said,

"Roll over, roll over."

So they all rolled over and one fell out.

There was one in the bed and the little one said,

"Goodnight!"

Food
Rhymes

Hot Cross Buns!

Hot cross buns!

Hot cross buns!

One a penny, two a penny,

Hot cross buns!

If you have no daughters,

Give them to your sons.

One a penny, two a penny,

Hot cross buns!

Catch It If You Can

Mix a pancake,
Beat a pancake,
Put it in a pan.
Cook a pancake,
Toss a pancake,
Catch it if you can!

Simple Simon

Simple Simon met a pieman going to the fair;

Said Simple Simon to the pieman,

"Let me taste your ware."

Said the pieman to Simple Simon,

"Show me first your penny."

Said Simple Simon to the pieman,

"Sir, I have not any!"

Do You Know the Muffin Man?

Oh, do you know the muffin man,
The muffin man, the muffin man?
Oh, do you know the muffin man,
That lives on Drury Lane?

Oh yes, I know the muffin man,
The muffin man, the muffin man!
Oh yes, I know the muffin man,
That lives on Drury Lane!

Georgie Porgie

Georgie Porgie, pudding and pie,
Kissed the girls, and made them cry.
When the boys came out to play,
Georgie Porgie ran away.

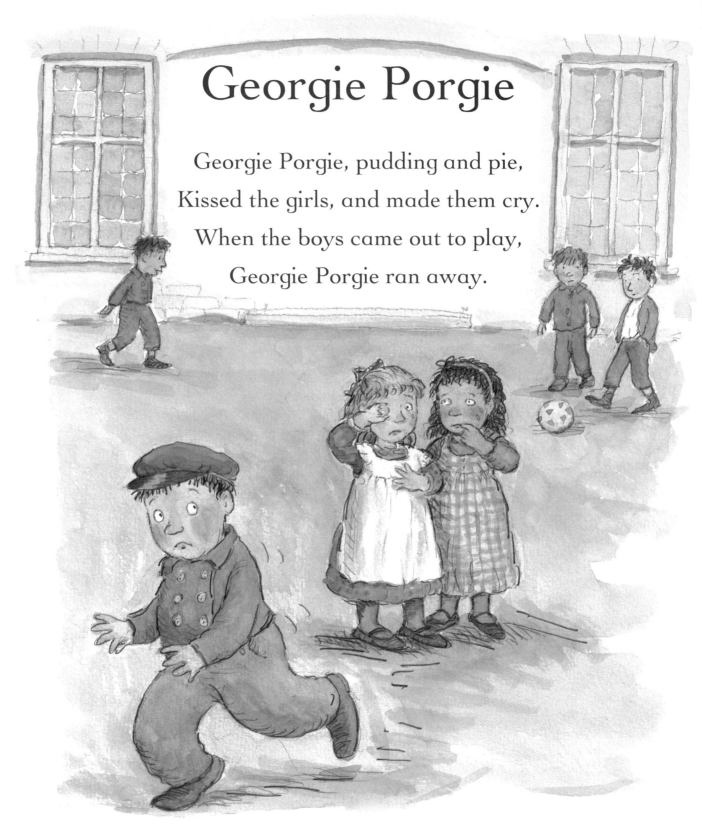

Jack Sprat

Jack Sprat could eat no fat,

His wife could eat no lean;

And so, between the two of them,

They licked the platter clean.

Little Jack Horner

Little Jack Horner sat in the corner,

Eating his Christmas pie;

He put in his thumb, and pulled out a plum,

And said, "What a good boy am I!"

Little Tommy Tucker

Little Tommy Tucker sings for his supper,

What shall we give him? Brown bread and butter.

How shall he cut it without a knife?

How shall he marry without a wife?

Oats and Beans and Barley Grow

Oats and beans and barley grow,

Oats and beans and barley grow.

Do you or I or anyone know

How oats and beans and barley grow?

First the farmer sows his seed,

Then he stands and takes his ease.

Stamps his feet and claps his hands

And turns around to view the lands.

Oats and beans and barley grow,

Oats and beans and barley grow.

Do you or I or anyone know

How oats and beans and barley grow?

Animal Rhymes

Little Bo-Peep

Little Bo-Peep has lost her sheep,

And doesn't know where to find them;

Leave them alone,

and they'll come home,

Wagging their tails behind them.

Mary Had a Little Lamb

Mary had a little lamb,
Its fleece was white as snow;
And everywhere that Mary went
The lamb was sure to go.

It followed her to school one day,
Which was against the rule;
It made the children laugh and play
To see a lamb at school.

Little Boy Blue

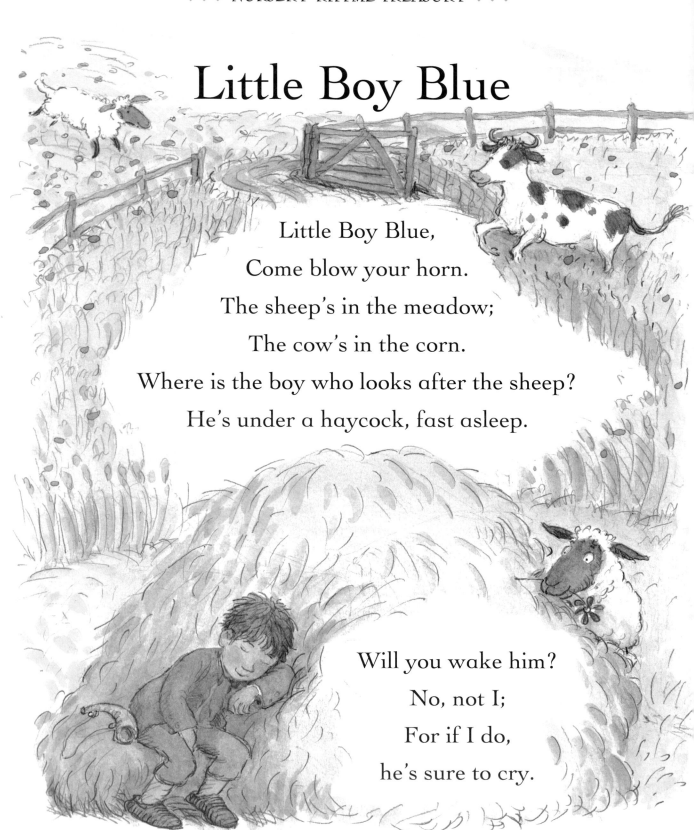

Little Boy Blue,
Come blow your horn.
The sheep's in the meadow;
The cow's in the corn.
Where is the boy who looks after the sheep?
He's under a haycock, fast asleep.

Will you wake him?
No, not I;
For if I do,
he's sure to cry.

Baa, Baa, Black Sheep

Baa, baa, black sheep,
Have you any wool?
Yes sir, yes sir,
Three bags full.
One for the master,
And one for the dame,
And one for the little boy
Who lives down the lane.

Cock-a-Doodle-Doo!

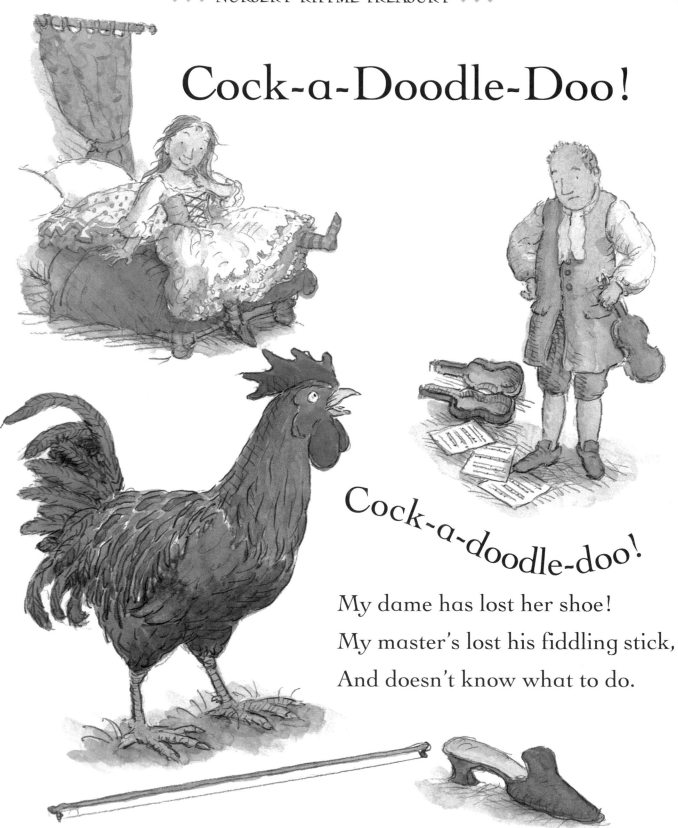

Cock-a-doodle-doo!

My dame has lost her shoe!

My master's lost his fiddling stick,

And doesn't know what to do.

Goosey, Goosey, Gander

Goosey, goosey, gander,

Whither do you wander?

Upstairs and downstairs

And in my lady's chamber.

There I met an old man

Who would not say his prayers,

So I took him by the left leg,

And threw him down the stairs.

Hickety Pickety

Hickety Pickety, my black hen,
She lays eggs for gentlemen;
Sometimes nine, and sometimes ten,
Hickety Pickety, my black hen!

I Had a Little Hen

I had a little hen,
    the prettiest ever seen,
She washed up the dishes,
    and kept the house clean.

She went to the mill
    to fetch me some flour,
And always got home
    in less than an hour.

She baked me my bread,
    she brewed me my ale,
She sat by the fire
    and told a fine tale!

Ding Dong Bell

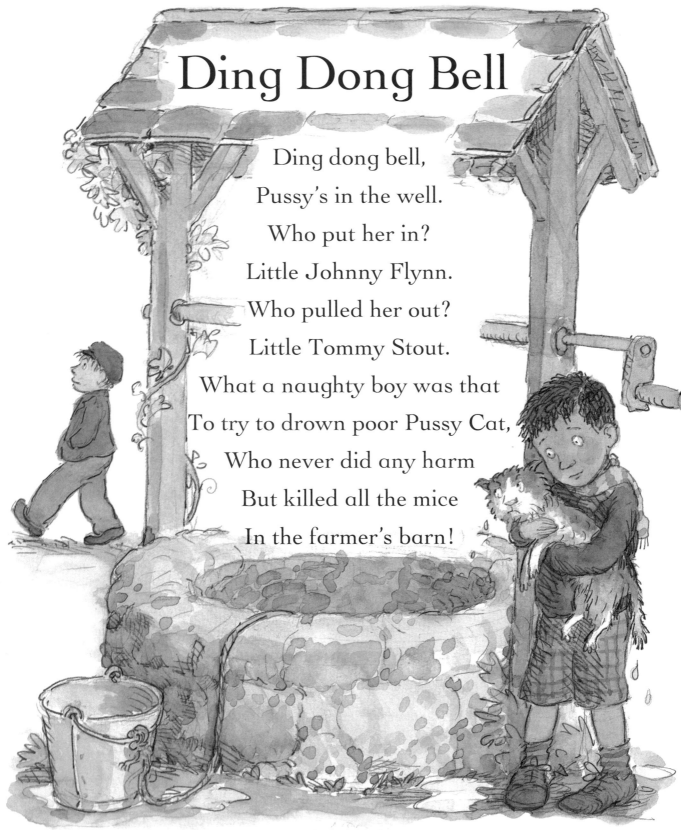

Ding dong bell,

Pussy's in the well.

Who put her in?

Little Johnny Flynn.

Who pulled her out?

Little Tommy Stout.

What a naughty boy was that

To try to drown poor Pussy Cat,

Who never did any harm

But killed all the mice

In the farmer's barn!

Pussy Cat, Pussy Cat

Pussy cat, pussy cat,
where have you been?
I've been to London
to visit the Queen.
Pussy cat, pussy cat,
what did you there?
I frightened a little mouse
under her chair.

Hey Diddle Diddle

Hey diddle diddle, the cat and the fiddle,

The cow jumped over the moon.

The little dog laughed to see such fun

And the dish ran away with the spoon!

Hickory, Dickory, Dock

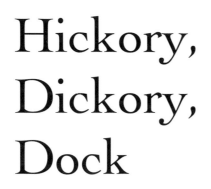

Hickory, dickory, dock,
The mouse ran up the clock.
The clock struck one,
The mouse ran down,
Hickory, dickory, dock.

Three Blind Mice

Three blind mice, three blind mice,
See how they run, see how they run!
They all ran after the farmer's wife,
Who cut off their tails with a carving knife,
Did you ever see such a thing in your life
As three blind mice?

Old Mother Hubbard

Old Mother Hubbard
Went to the cupboard,
To get her poor doggie a bone;

But when she got there
The cupboard was bare,
So her poor little doggie had none.

Higglety, Pigglety, Pop!

Higglety, pigglety, pop!

The dog has eaten the mop;

The pig's in a hurry,

The cat's in a flurry,

Higglety, pigglety, POP!

Little Robin Redbreast

Little Robin Redbreast sat upon a tree,
Up went Pussy Cat, and down went he!
Down came Pussy, and away Robin ran;
Says little Robin Redbreast,
"Catch me if you can!"

Miaow

Little Robin Redbreast
flew upon a wall,
Pussy Cat jumped after him,
and almost had a fall!
Little Robin chirped and sang,
and what did Pussy say?
Pussy Cat said, "Miaow,"
and Robin flew away.

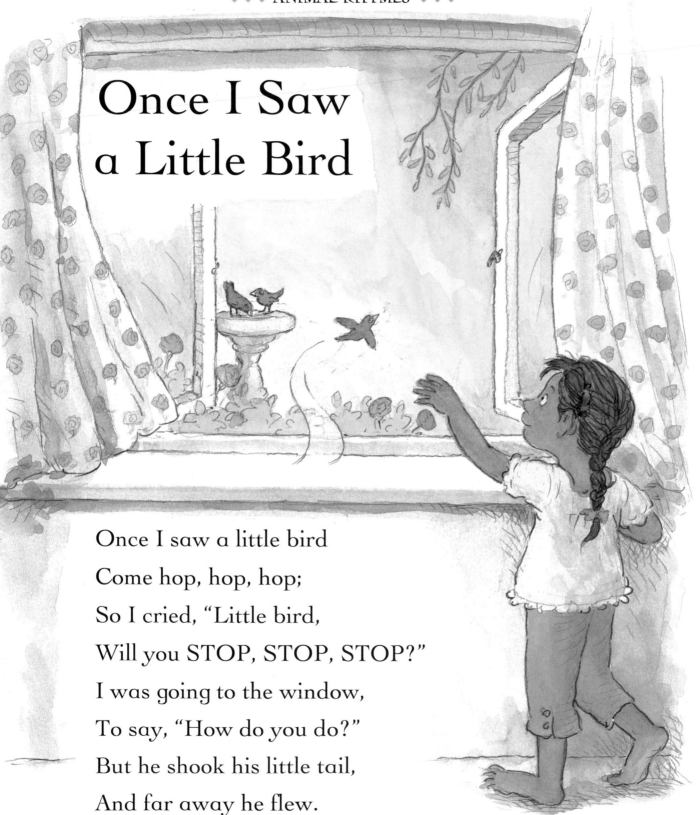

Once I Saw a Little Bird

Once I saw a little bird
Come hop, hop, hop;
So I cried, "Little bird,
Will you STOP, STOP, STOP?"
I was going to the window,
To say, "How do you do?"
But he shook his little tail,
And far away he flew.

Horsie, Horsie

Horsie, horsie, don't you stop,
Just let your feet go clippety clop;
Your tail goes swish,
And the wheels go round;
Giddy-up, you're homeward bound!

I Had a Little Hobby-Horse

I had a little hobby-horse,
And it was dapple grey;
Its head was made of pea-straw,
Its tail was made of hay.

I sold it to an old woman
For a copper groat;
And I'll not sing my song again
Without another coat.

The Owl and the Pussy Cat

The Owl and the Pussy Cat went to sea

In a beautiful pea-green boat,

They took some honey, and plenty of money,

Wrapped up in a five pound note.

The Owl looked up to the stars above,

And sang to a small guitar,

"Oh lovely Pussy! Oh Pussy, my love,

What a beautiful Pussy you are, you are, you are,

What a beautiful Pussy you are."

Pussy said to the Owl, "You elegant fowl,

How charmingly sweet you sing.

Oh let us be married, too long we have tarried;

But what shall we do for a ring?"

They sailed away, for a year and a day,

To the land where the Bong-tree grows,

And there in a wood a Piggy-wig stood

With a ring at the end of his nose, his nose, his nose,

With a ring at the end of his nose.

"Dear Pig, are you willing to sell for one shilling your ring?"

Said the Piggy, "I will."

So they took it away, and were married next day

By the Turkey who lives on the hill.

They dined on mince, and slices of quince,

Which they ate with a runcible spoon.

And hand in hand, on the edge of the sand.

They danced by the light of the moon, the moon, the moon,

They danced by the light of the moon.

Nonsense

Rhymes

Diddle Diddle Dumpling

Diddle, diddle, dumpling, my son John,

Went to bed with his trousers on;

One shoe off, and the other shoe on,

Diddle, diddle, dumpling, my son John.

It's Raining, It's Pouring

It's raining, it's pouring,

The old man is snoring.

He went to bed and he bumped his head,

And couldn't get up in the morning.

Vintery, Mintery

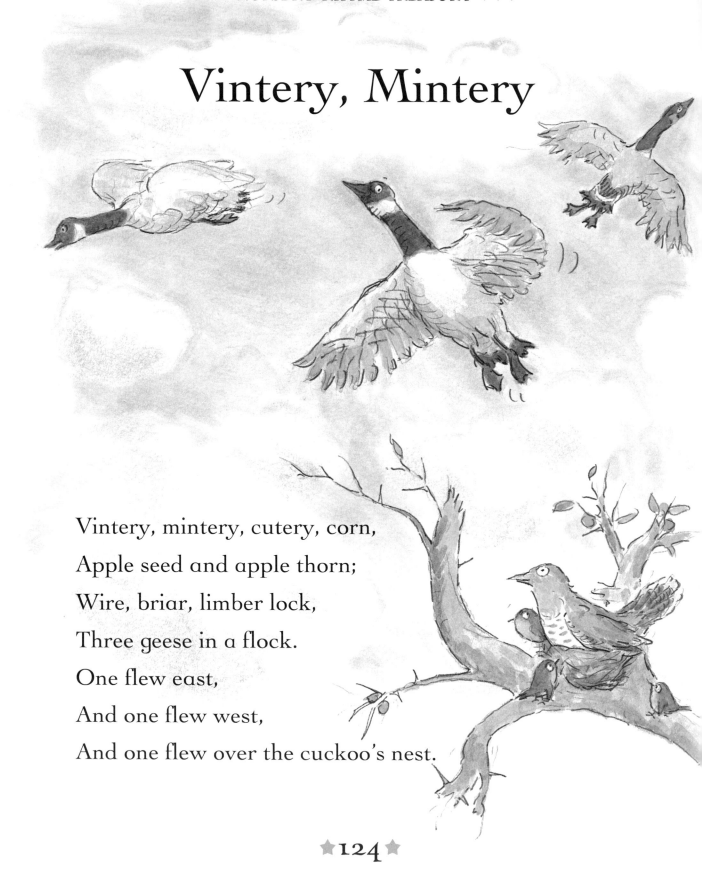

Vintery, mintery, cutery, corn,

Apple seed and apple thorn;

Wire, briar, limber lock,

Three geese in a flock.

One flew east,

And one flew west,

And one flew over the cuckoo's nest.

Pop Goes the Weasel

Half a pound of tuppenny rice,

Half a pound of treacle.

That's the way the money goes,

Pop goes the weasel!

Up and down the city road,

In and out of the Eagle,

That's the way the money goes,

Pop goes the weasel!

There Was a Crooked Man

There was a crooked man
and he walked a crooked mile,

He found a crooked sixpence
upon a crooked stile;

He bought a crooked cat,
which caught a crooked mouse,

And they all lived together
in a little crooked house.

There Was an Old Man Called Michael Finnegan

There was an old man called Michael Finnegan

He grew whiskers on his chinnegan.

Along came the wind and blew them in again

Poor old Michael Finnegan.

Begin again.

What Are Little Boys Made Of?

What are little boys made of?

What are little boys made of?

Slugs and snails,

And puppy-dogs' tails,

That's what little boys are made of.

What Are Little Girls Made Of?

What are little girls made of?
What are little girls made of?
Sugar and spice,
And all things nice,
That's what little girls are made of.

Tweedledum and Tweedledee

Tweedledum and Tweedledee
Agreed to have a battle;
For Tweedledum said Tweedledee
Had spoiled his nice new rattle.

Just then flew down a monstrous crow,
As black as a tar-barrel;
Which frightened both the heroes so,
They quite forgot their quarrel.

Robin and Richard

Robin and Richard were two pretty men,

They lay in bed till the clock struck ten;

Then up starts Robin, and looks at the sky,

"Oh! Oh! brother Richard, the sun's very high,

You go before with bottle and bag,

And I'll follow after on little Jack Nag."

Little Nancy Etticoat

Little Nancy Etticoat,
In a white petticoat,
And a red rose.
The longer she stands,
The shorter she grows.

What is she?
(Riddle answer: A candle)

As I Was Going to St Ives

As I was going to St Ives,

I met a man with seven wives.

Each wife had seven sacks;

Each sack had seven cats;

Each cat had seven kits.

Kits, cats, sacks and wives.

How many were going to St Ives?

(Riddle answer: Just one person is going to St Ives)

Aiken Drum

There was a man lived in the moon,
Lived in the moon, lived in the moon.
There was a man lived in the moon,
And his name was Aiken Drum.

And he played upon a ladle,
A ladle, a ladle,
And he played upon a ladle,
And his name was Aiken Drum.

And his hat was made of good cream cheese,
Of good cream cheese, of good cream cheese,
And his hat was made of good cream cheese,
And his name was Aiken Drum.

And his coat was made of good roast beef,
Of good roast beef, of good roast beef,
And his coat was made of good roast beef,
And his name was Aiken Drum.

And his buttons were made of penny loaves,
Of penny loaves, of penny loaves,
And his buttons were made of penny loaves,
And his name was Aiken Drum.

And his breeches were made of haggis bags,
Of haggis bags, of haggis bags,
And his breeches were made of haggis bags,
And his name was Aiken Drum.

The House that Jack Built

This is the house that Jack built.

This is the malt
That lay in the house that Jack built.

This is the rat,
That ate the malt
That lay in the house that Jack built.

This is the cat,
That killed the rat,
That ate the malt
That lay in the house that Jack built.

This is the dog,
That worried the cat,
That killed the rat,
That ate the malt
That lay in the house that Jack built.

This is the cow with the crumpled horn,

That tossed the dog,

That worried the cat,

That killed the rat,

That ate the malt

That lay in the house that Jack built.

This is the maiden all forlorn,

That milked the cow with the crumpled horn,

That tossed the dog,

That worried the cat,

That killed the rat,

That ate the malt

That lay in the house that Jack built.

This is the man all tattered and torn,

That kissed the maiden all forlorn,

That milked the cow with the crumpled horn,

That tossed the dog,

That worried the cat,

That killed the rat,

That ate the malt

That lay in the house that Jack built.

This is the priest all shaven and shorn,

That married the man all tattered and torn,

That kissed the maiden all forlorn,

That milked the cow with the crumpled horn,

That tossed the dog,

That worried the cat,

That killed the rat,

That ate the malt

That lay in the house that Jack built.

This is the cock that crowed in the morn,

That waked the priest all shaven and shorn,

That married the man all tattered and torn,

That kissed the maiden all forlorn,

That milked the cow with the crumpled horn,

That tossed the dog,

That worried the cat,

That killed the rat,

That ate the malt

That lay in the house that Jack built.

This is the farmer sowing his corn,

That kept the cock that crowed in the morn,

That waked the priest all shaven and shorn,

That married the man all tattered and torn,

That kissed the maiden all forlorn,

That milked the cow with the crumpled horn,

That tossed the dog,

That worried the cat,

That killed the rat,

That ate the malt

That lay in the house that Jack built.

Three Young Rats

Three young rats with black felt hats,

Three young ducks with white straw flats,

Three young dogs with curling tails,

Three young cats with demi-veils,

Went out to walk with two young pigs

In satin vests and sorrel wigs,

But suddenly it chanced to rain

And so they all went home again.

Playground

Rhymes

This is the way we mend our clothes,
Mend our clothes, mend our clothes.
This is the way we mend our clothes,
On a cold and frosty morning.

This is the way we sweep the floor,
Sweep the floor, sweep the floor.
This is the way we sweep the floor,
On a cold and frosty morning.

This is the way we bake our bread,
Bake our bread, bake our bread.
This is the way we bake our bread,
On a cold and frosty morning.

This is the way we get dressed up,
Get dressed up, get dressed up.
This is the way we get dressed up,
On a cold and frosty morning.

Ring-a-Ring o' Roses

Ring-a-ring o' roses,

A pocket full of posies.

A-tishoo! A-tishoo!

We all fall down.

Miss Mary Mack

Miss Mary Mack,

All dressed in black,

With silver buttons,

All down her back,

She asked her mother,

For fifty cents,

To see the elephant,
Jump the fence,
They jumped so high,
They touched the sky,
And didn't come back,
Till the fourth of July.

The Big Ship Sails

The big ship sails on the ally-ally-oh,
The ally-ally-oh, the ally-ally-oh.
Oh, the big ship sails on the ally-ally-oh
On the last day of September.

The captain said it will never, never do,
Never, never do, never, never do.
The captain said it will never, never do
On the last day of September.

The big ship sank to the bottom of the sea,
The bottom of the sea, the bottom of the sea.
The big ship sank to the bottom of the sea
On the last day of September.

We all dip our heads in the deep blue sea,
The deep blue sea, the deep blue sea.
We all dip our heads in the deep blue sea
On the last day of September.

The Farmer's in his Den

The farmer's in his den,

The farmer's in his den,

E I E I O—

The farmer's in his den.

The farmer wants a wife,
The farmer wants a wife,
E I E I O—
The farmer wants a wife.

The wife wants a child,
The wife wants a child,
E I E I O—
The wife wants a child.

The child wants a nurse,
The child wants a nurse,
E I E I O—
The child wants a nurse.

The nurse wants a dog,
The nurse wants a dog,
E I E I O—
The nurse wants a dog.

The dog wants a bone,

The dog wants a bone,

E I E I O—

The dog wants a bone.

We all pat the bone,

We all pat the bone,

E I E I O—

We all pat the bone.

Sing a Song of Sixpence

Sing a song of sixpence
    A pocket full of rye;
Four and twenty blackbirds
    Baked in a pie.
When the pie was opened
    The birds began to sing;
Now wasn't that a dainty dish
    To set before the king?

The king was in his counting house
    Counting out his money;
The queen was in the parlour
    Eating bread and honey.
The maid was in the garden
    Hanging out the clothes,
When down came a blackbird
    And pecked off her nose!

The Queen of Hearts

The Queen of Hearts, she made some tarts

All on a summer's day.

The Knave of Hearts, he stole the tarts

And took them clean away.

The King of Hearts, called for the tarts

And beat the Knave full sore.

The Knave of Hearts, brought back the tarts

And vowed he'd steal no more.

Oranges and Lemons

Oranges and lemons,

Say the bells of St. Clements.

You owe me five farthings,

Say the bells of St. Martins.

When will you pay me?

Say the bells of Old Bailey.

When I grow rich,

Say the bells of Shoreditch.

When will that be?

Say the bells of Stepney.

I do not know,

Says the great bell at Bow.

Here comes a candle to light you to bed,

Here comes a chopper to chop off your head.

Chip chop, chip chop, the last man's head.

A Sailor Went to Sea

A sailor went to sea, sea, sea.
To see what he could see, see, see.
But all that he could see, see, see.
Was the bottom of the deep blue sea, sea, sea.

Have you ever, ever, ever,
in your long-legged life
met a long-legged sailor
with a long-legged wife?

No, I never, never, never,
in my long-legged life
met a long-legged sailor
with a long-legged wife.

Have you ever, ever, ever,
in your short-legged life...

Have you ever, ever, ever,
in your knock-kneed life...

Have you ever, ever, ever,
in your pigeon-toed life...

Have you ever, ever, ever,
in your bow-legged life...

I Had a Little Puppy

I had a little puppy
His name was Tiny Tim
I put him in the bathtub,
To see if he could swim.

He drank all the water,
He ate a bar of soap
The next thing you know
He had a bubble in his throat.

In came the doctor,

In came the nurse,

In came the lady with the alligator purse.

Out went the doctor

Out went the nurse

Out went the lady with the alligator purse.

The Lion and the Unicorn

The lion and the unicorn were fighting for the crown;

The lion beat the unicorn all around the town.

Some gave them white bread,

and some gave them brown;

Some gave them plum cake,

and drummed them out of town.

Bedtime
Rhymes

Bedtime

The evening is coming, the sun sinks to rest;
The rooks are all flying straight home to the nest.
"Caw!" says the rook, as he flies overhead;
"It's time little people were going to bed!"

The flowers are closing; the daisy's asleep;

The primrose is buried in slumber so deep.

Shut up for the night is the pimpernel red;

It's time little people were going to bed!

The butterfly, drowsy, has folded its wing;

The bees are returning, no more the birds sing.

Their labour is over, their nestlings are fed;

It's time little people were going to bed!

Come to Bed, Says Sleepy-Head

"Come to bed," says Sleepy-head;

"Tarry a while," says Slow;

"Put on the pot," says Greedy-gut,

"Let's sup before we go."

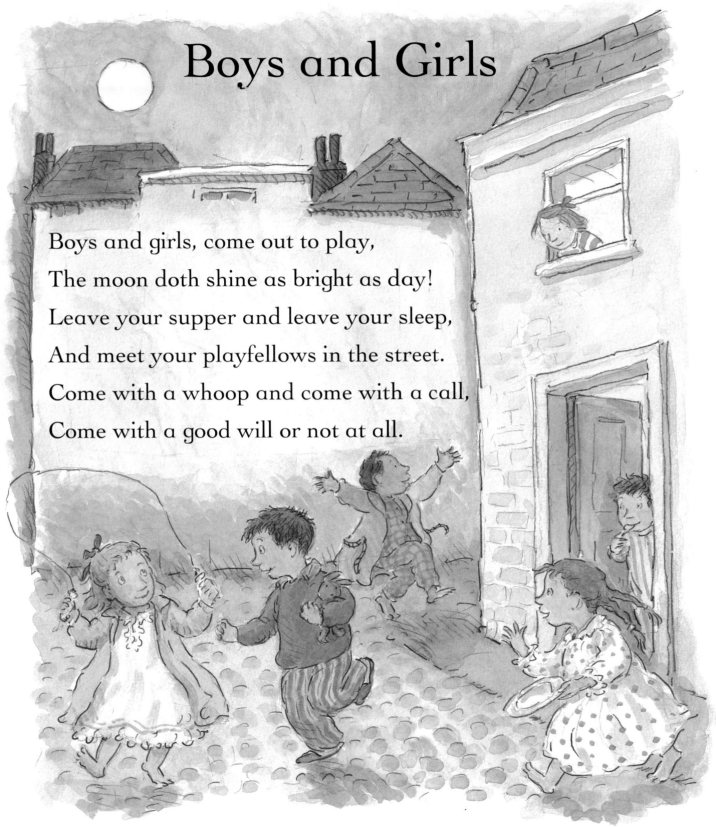

Boys and Girls

Boys and girls, come out to play,

The moon doth shine as bright as day!

Leave your supper and leave your sleep,

And meet your playfellows in the street.

Come with a whoop and come with a call,

Come with a good will or not at all.

Bed in Summer

In winter I get up at night,

And dress by yellow candle-light.

In summer, quite the other way,

I have to go to bed by day.

I have to go to bed and see

The birds still hopping on the tree,

Or hear the grown-up people's feet

Still going past me in the street.

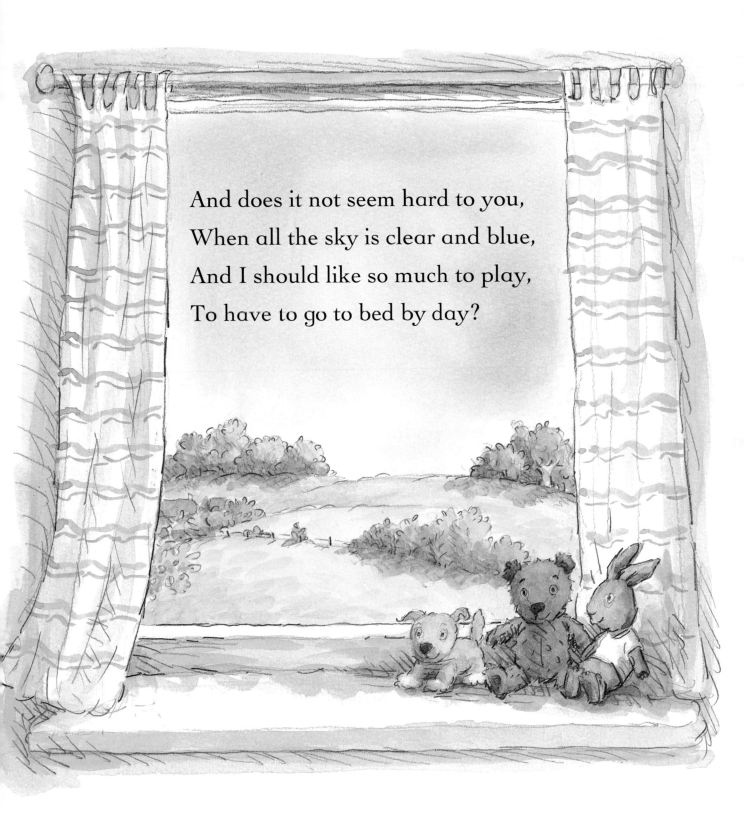

And does it not seem hard to you,
When all the sky is clear and blue,
And I should like so much to play,
To have to go to bed by day?

Brahms' Lullaby

Lullaby, and good night,
With rosy bed light,
With lilies overspread,
Is my baby's sweet bed.

Lay you down now, and rest,
May your slumber be blessed!
Lay you down now, and rest,
May your slumber be blessed!

Lullaby, and good night,
You're your mother's delight,
Shining angels beside
My darling abide.

Soft and warm is your bed,

Close your eyes and rest your head.

Soft and warm is your bed,

Close your eyes and rest your head.

Twinkle, Twinkle, Little Star

Twinkle, twinkle, little star,
How I wonder what you are!
Up above the world so high,
Like a diamond in the sky.

When the blazing sun is gone,
When he nothing shines upon,
Then you show your little light,
Twinkle, twinkle all the night.

Then the traveller in the dark,
Thanks you for your tiny spark,
He could not see which way to go,
If you did not twinkle so.

In the dark blue sky you keep,
And often through my curtains peep,
For you never shut your eye,
Till the sun is in the sky.

As your bright and tiny spark,
Lights the traveller in the dark –
Though I know not what you are,
Twinkle, twinkle, little star.

Go to Bed First

Go to bed first,
A golden purse;

Go to bed second,
A golden pheasant;

Go to bed third,
A golden bird.

Go to Bed Late

Go to bed late,
Stay very small;
Go to bed early,
Grow very tall.

Go to Bed, Tom

Go to bed, Tom,
Go to bed, Tom,
Tired or not, Tom,
Go to bed, Tom.

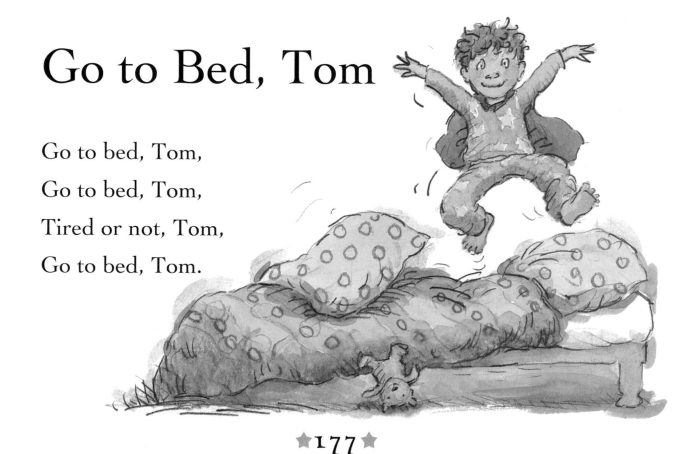

Now the Day is Over

Now the day is over,
Night is drawing nigh,
Shadows of the evening
Steal across the sky.

Now the darkness gathers,
Stars begin to peep,
Birds and beasts and flowers
Soon will be asleep.

Golden Slumbers

Golden slumbers kiss your eyes,
Smiles await you when you rise;
Sleep, pretty baby, do not cry,
And I will sing a lullaby.

Bye, Baby Bunting

Bye, baby bunting,
Daddy's gone a-hunting,
Gone to get a rabbit-skin,
To wrap my baby bunting in.

Wee Willie Winkie

Wee Willie Winkie
Runs through the town,
Upstairs and downstairs
In his nightgown.
Rapping at the window,
Crying through the lock,
Are the children all in bed?
It's past eight o' clock.

How Many Miles to Babylon?

How many miles to Babylon?

Three score and ten.

Can I get there by candle-light?

Yes, and back again.

If your heels are nimble and light,

You may get there by candle-light.

Hush Little Baby

Hush little baby, don't say a word,
Papa's gonna buy you a mocking bird.

If that mocking bird don't sing,
Papa's gonna buy you a diamond ring.

If that diamond ring turns to brass,
Papa's gonna buy you a looking-glass.

If that looking-glass gets broke,
Papa's gonna buy you a billy goat.

If that billy goat don't pull,
Papa's gonna buy you a cart and mule.

If that cart and mule turn over,
Papa's gonna buy you a dog named Rover.

If that dog named Rover won't bark,
Papa's gonna buy you a horse and cart.

If that horse and cart fall down,
You'll still be the sweetest little baby
in town.

Little Fred

When little Fred went to bed,
He always said his prayers;
He kissed Mama, and then Papa,
And straightaway went upstairs.

Rock-a-Bye, Baby

Rock-a-bye, baby, on the tree top,

When the wind blows, the cradle will rock;

When the bough breaks, the cradle will fall,

Down will come baby, cradle and all.

Jack Be Nimble

Jack be nimble,
Jack be quick,
Jack jump over
The candlestick.

Star Light, Star Bright

Star light, star bright,
First star I see tonight,
I wish I may, I wish I might,
Have the wish I wish tonight.

Sleep Little Child

Sleep little child, go to sleep,
Mother is here by your bed.
Sleep little child, go to sleep,
Rest on the pillow your head.

The world is silent and still,
The moon shines bright on the hill,
Then creeps past the window sill.

Sleep little child, go to sleep,
Oh sleep, go to sleep.

Index of First Lines